somersaulted into a huge, black pot over a fire.

"Well, Leonardo!" mocked Shredder's. "What a disastrous leader you turned out to be!"

The last thing Leonardo remembered was lunging towards Shredder in an effort to reclaim his title as leader of the Teenage Mutant Hero Turtles…

Then he was back in their underground lair, eyes wide with fear, face covered with sweat.

"Huh?" He looked around in a daze, raising a flipper to his head. "What a nightmare!"

He tried to sleep again, but it was impossible. All through the night he was haunted by a nagging fear. Could such a nightmare be an omen for the future? Again and again, he comforted himself with the thought that things would seem different in the day time. But he didn't really feel any better.

"What's wrong, Leonardo?" said Donatello next morning.

"That dream…" Leonardo was almost speaking to himself. "I feel it was a warning that my judgement is beginning to fail!"

"You'll be just fine!" grinned Donatello, not really listening. "Come on, let's practise!"

Without thinking, Leonardo brought his sword straight up - with the result that it smashed straight into his own forehead and snapped into two pieces! The Turtles could see their leader was badly shaken.

TEENAGE MUTANT *HERO*
TURTLES™

FOLLOW
MY LEADER

Written by Maureen Spurgeon
Illustrated by Clic Publishing

LEONARDO knew something was wrong. So many times he had led the Teenage Mutant Hero Turtles against the evil Shredder from Dimension X. Why was it that, now, he just wanted to turn away and forget everything?

"Let's take them!" Raphael's shout seemed to thud in his brain. The images of Bebop, the half-human, half-rhino minder, and his semi-warthog pal, Rocksteady, blurred together.

"What's the plan, Leonardo?" urged Michaelangelo.

Leonardo's heart beat faster. He swallowed hard. "Well, we could cut to the left..." he faltered, looking around. "Or, maybe to the right... I - I can't decide!"

"You're a great help!" snapped Raphael, pushing him out of the way.

Leonardo could only watch the whole, crazy episode that followed. Donatello got tangled up in Bebop's spaghetti dinner, while Michaelangelo fell through a trap door hidden in a giant pizza!

"Set loose the vicious dogs!" barked Shredder. Leonardo's mouth went dry. Next minute, two toy poodles came charging out. They barked and snapped at his feet, making him retreat - until he finally

"My judgement is gone," he kept saying. "I'm not fit to lead anyone."

"Hey - everyone goofs up once in a while!" comforted Michaelangelo.

"After all," added Raphael, "Turtles are only human!"

But it was no good - Leonardo had made up his mind. "I've thought about it," he said, "and I must leave!"

Raphael, Donatello and Michaelangelo all rushed after him. But, by the time they had pushed up the nearest manhole cover and peered out into the street, Leonardo had gone. There was only a howling gust of wind whipping past them.

"Brrr!" exclaimed Michaelangelo, with a shiver. "It's cold!" He pointed up at the sky. "Scope that out, dudes!"

"Is my eyesight going," Raphael wondered, following the direction of Michaelangelo's flipper, "or is the sun getting smaller?"

"Scientifically impossible!" pronounced Donatello firmly. But, even as he spoke, white, feathery flakes began drifting down!

"This is totally nutzoid!" Michaelangelo burst out. "Now, it's snowing!"

Something unusual was also happening on the other side of town. A four foot tall robot was rolling towards an empty skyscraper building and it was being controlled by someone carrying a huge dish antenna - someone with a steel helmet and visor!

"That's far enough!" growled Shredder. The robot stopped. "Nobody in uniform - and definitely no Turtles - must enter the building!"

In reply, a formidable collection of blades and weapons flicked out of the robot body, making it look like a gigantic multi-blade penknife!

"This had better work, Shredder!" barked Krang, the pink, rubbery features of the Dimension X dictator speaking from the centre of his walking body. Together, they carried the dish antenna into the skyscraper.

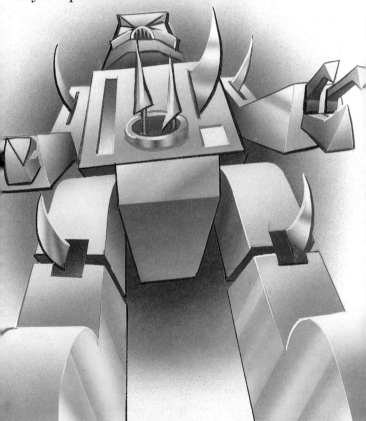

Next minute a police car drew up. "There's the tower block!" shouted a policeman, squinting through the falling snow. "What's up?"

"I don't know!" admitted his companion. "Something about a robot barricading the entrance!" Three armed policemen jumped out and ran towards the building.

"Uniforms…" droned Shredder's robot, a revolving red light flashing away on its head. "Uniforms! Entrance denied!"

The police didn't know what hit them! Half a dozen arms sprang out, one holding a gigantic pair of handcuffs, another a bola rope with weights at one end - there was even a catapult with the elastic band pulled back, ready to fire! Within seconds the policemen were well and truly immobilised.

By this time Krang and Shredder had arrived at the top level of the skyscraper, ready to link up control base to the dish antenna which they positioned in front of an open window.

"What's taking so long, Shredder?" barked Krang. The device crackled with energy and it was getting on his nerves.

"Patience, Krang!" Shredder adjusted the dish for the last time, his steely eyes glittering. Now Krang could see the antenna drawing in energy to the control base. It travelled along some heavy cables which in turn led into a cluster of giant batteries! "My solar syphon will soon drain all the energy from the sun and store it in these solar batteries!"

"Which means," Krang broke in, "we shall have the power of the sun at our disposal!"

"While the entire planet is turned into a deep freeze that will make the Ice Age seem like a Turkish bath!" finished Shredder.

Of course, the Turtles were unaware of Shredder's latest plan. In any case, Leonardo's disappearance worried them far more than the unusually cold weather.

"This is a lesson in life, my students," Splinter told them. "Each of you must learn from it."

"So, like," gulped Michaelangelo, "who's going to be leader?"

"Maybe we could toss up for it..." mused Donatello.

"Better than that!" cried Raphael, snapping his fingers. "We'll spin the pizza!" They all crouched down on the floor around a large tray with a single piece of pizza on it. Raphael set it spinning around.

Slowly, the spinning tray came to a stop - with the slice pointing at Raphael!

"Looks like you're it, Raphael!" announced Donatello. "So, what do we do, now?"

"Uh?" Raphael was beginning to wish he'd hit on another idea. "I dunno. Go up top and look around?"

He led the way to the manhole cover and pushed hard against it.

"Ugh!" he grunted. "It's stuck!"

"Allow me!" said Donatello, raising one end of his sword and giving an almighty heave.

It took quite a while, but at last the cover flew off with a loud clang, sending down a mini mountain of snow on to the Turtles' heads!

"What now, Leader?" enquired Michaelangelo.

"When in doubt," said Raphael, "climb on out!" The other two followed him up to the road, their eyes widening when they got there.

"Oh, man!" breathed Michaelangelo, looking around at the white world. "Dig all this snow!"

"It looks exactly like the North Pole!" commented Donatello.

"You're just saying that because of the polar bear!" Michaelangelo chipped in. Donatello and Raphael followed his gaze, hardly able to believe their eyes. Sure enough there was a polar bear, with thick white fur, a massive head and gigantic paws...

"Guys!" choked Raphael. "I don't think I want to be leader any more!"

They started to run, slipping and slithering on the ice, then ploughing into a group of penguins, sending them flying!

"I've never fought a polar bear before!" gasped Raphael. "What do I do?"

Something had to be done, and fast! With a roar, the bear was coming right at them, its huge mouth open wide enough for the Turtles to see every one of its razor sharp teeth!

"Look, fella!" yelled Michaelangelo. As the Polar Bear looked up, Michaelangelo broke off a piece of ice from a frozen water fountain - a piece of ice with a fish inside!

The bear caught the fish in its mouth, gulping it down in one swallow.

"Come on, amigos!" yelled Michaelangelo, seeing their chance to make a getaway. "Let's make Turtle tracks!"

The Turtles were more than ready! They cleared the water fountain at breakneck speed and clambered over an iron fence, knowing that the polar bear was safely behind them!

"Look!" yelled Donatello, pointing to a line of snow-covered cages. "Raphael - you brought us up into the middle of the zoo!"

"Well, it's free isn't it?" Raphael defended himself.

"Chill out, you dudes!" Michaelangelo cut in. "We've got to work out what's making the sun shrink!"

"It's obvious that something is draining its solar energy and substance," explained the brainy Donatello, calmly taking out a metal box with a screen on it. "We can use this Energy Tracker I invented to lead us to the source of the trouble!"

"That does it!" snapped Raphael. "You have all the answers - you be the leader!"

"All right!" retorted Donatello and switched on the device, studying the diagram which appeared on the screen.

"The source of the solar drain is due east of here. But first we have to calculate the vector co-ordinates in order to triangulate the correct route!"

"You said it was east!" interrupted Raphael. "So, let's go east!"

"Look," Donatello rounded on him, "I'm leader, and we're going to do it my way!"

Shredder was congratulating himself on his success. Giant sparks and crackles of energy continued travelling into the deadly solar syphon in a most satisfying way!

"The solar batteries are nearly full!" cackled Krang, "and the sun is draining rapidly!"

"Excellent!" Shredder chimed in. "Soon, every living being on this planet will be frozen!" He rubbed his hands together with relish. "We'll thaw them out as we need them! The people of Earth will be our willing slaves!"

All this time, Donatello had been busy working out the plans and diagrams on his Energy Tracker. But where did his calculations lead the Turtles? To a quaint-looking old school house, complete with bell turret!

Still, Raphael and Michaelangelo thought to themselves, Donatello was the leader...

Inside, everything was covered with ice. And when Michaelangelo slammed the door shut, there was an avalanche of snow crashed down from the roof, blocking the door!

"Great!" growled Donatello. "Now we're trapped in here!"

"Still," he went on, brightening up a little, "once we put that solar device out of action, all the snow will thaw! According to the Energy Tracker, it's up in the bell tower!"

Getting upstairs would have been impossible without their mountain climbing gear - the ice was inches thick on every step.

When they finally reached the top, there was nothing in the tower but a large bell and a small black box with two lights on it…

"That's what is shrinking the sun?" queried Raphael.

"Uh, no…" said Donatello, hesitating a little. "Actually, it's something designed to trick my Energy Tracker into thinking it's what is shrinking the sun!" Raphael and Michaelangelo held their breath.

"And besides being a transmitter, it's also an explosive device, with a timer that's triggered when it's picked up!"

"Like," gulped Michaelangelo, "like you just did!"

"Some leader you turned out to be!" yelled Raphael. But, Donatello was determined to keep cool.

"Michaelangelo," he bellowed, pointing upwards, "cut that bell down!"

"I'm way ahead of you!" Michaelangelo threw his dagger and it sliced clean through the bell rope! With a deafening crash and a succession of clangs, the huge bell plunged down through the floors, leaving a gaping hole for Donatello to throw the black box into!

The bomb exploded the minute it hit the ground, shaking the entire building - but crumbling the ice and snow as well, along with the whole of the front wall!

"Whoooah!" cried the Turtles, swinging down on their ropes and mountain gear. "Look out below! Coming down!"

Outside, the expanse of snow and ice stretched further than ever. The daylight was fading fast, casting strange shadows over the white city landscape.

"Isn't it getting dark rather early?" said Raphael.

"According to that big office clock," said Donatello, with a brief glance, "it's only three in the afternoon!" He looked up at the sky. "The sun has shrunk so much, it looks the same size as the other stars!"

"Terrific!" growled Raphael, with a shiver. "Now, what?"

"No problem!" Donatello assured him. "My Energy Tracker should lead us straight to the draining device!" Once again, he pulled out the metal box - lots of wires and springs were spilling out of it!

"Don't worry!" he cried, racing off. "I've got another one back at the lair!"

Raphael and Michaelangelo looked at each other. "I hate to say this. But, I guess you're the leader, now!" said Raphael.

Neither said another word. But their thoughts turned to Leonardo, the one who had led them so bravely and so well in the past. Where was he right now, they wondered?

Leonardo was missing the other Turtles far more than he realised. He hated being on his own, plodding through the snow, with nothing but a long line of Turtle tracks to show for it.

"Don't go near the bridge!" an old, cracked voice warned. An elderly toll keeper hurried towards Leonardo, with strands of frost on his thick, wire-rimmed glasses and walrus moustache. "The snow's got it over-weighted!"

He had barely finished speaking when the sound of groaning metal echoed across the white wasteland. For a split second it was actually possible to see the bridge bending beneath the weight of the frozen snow, before it collapsed, crashing on to the frozen surface of the river below!

"See what I mean?" declared the old man.

"Everyone talks about the weather, but nobody's doing anything about it!" Angrily, he stamped his way back through the snow.

Leonardo watched him go. "He's right! The whole world's in danger, and all I've thought about is myself!"

Next minute he had turned around, retracing his own tracks.

He had no idea that Michaelangelo and Raphael were also searching for him - not that they were having much success...

"Let's face it," Michaelangelo sighed wearily. "We're never going to find Leonardo!"

"Or this mysterious device that's draining the sun's energy!" added Raphael.

"Oh," said Michaelangelo, perking up a little, "that part's easy! Look over there!"

Then Raphael knew they had to be hot on the trail of Shredder's solar syphon! The shower of sparks coming from the top of the skyscraper was a dead giveaway, besides being the only bit of warmth and light in the whole city!

"Michaelangelo," breathed Raphael, "you've found it!"

"Now," said Michaelangelo, becoming very business-like, "let me do the talking! I'm the leader, remember?"

Suddenly handcuffs, chains, bola ropes and a collection of other weapons came whizzing out of nowhere, missing them by centimetres!

"Turtles!" droned the robot. "Turtles! You will not pass!"

As leader, Michaelangelo knew there was only one thing to do - get back behind the nearest snow bank! "Then we surround the enemy with a two-pronged attack!" he told Raphael. "I saw it in a movie once!"

It sounded like a good idea, but the robot was not to be beaten that easily! A sensor light on top of its head soon homed on Raphael and its great iron chest opened wide!

"Uh-oh!" yelled Raphael, making a desperate attempt to dodge a gigantic steel fist. "Who programmed this robot - King Kong?"

The robot claw snatched Raphael into the air and held him there, his green legs wriggling.

Michaelangelo snatched up a dustbin lid and used it as a shield against the barrage of weapons which came flying towards him. Each one scored a direct hit, taking out chunks of the lid until there was hardly anything left!

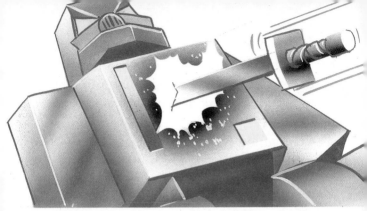

Then, just when it seemed they had no chance at all, a gleaming sword came flying through the air, hitting the circuit box on the back of the robot! There was a shower of sparks, a series of crackles and fizzes - and the steel enemy fell!

The Turtles knew only one person could throw like that!

"Leonardo!" cried Michaelangelo. "Great timing!"

"Oooof!" Raphael hit the ground with a thud after being released by the robot's claw. "Couldn't let a guy down easy, could you?"

"Hi, guys!" came another welcome voice, and Donatello appeared carrying the spare Energy Tracker! "Sorry I'm late!"

"The awesome foursome!" grinned Michaelangelo, flinging his arms around the other three Turtles. "How did you find us, Donatello?"

"Simple! I determined the co-efficient of energy, triangulated the approximate location, co-ordinated it with the grid..." Donatello took a deep breath. "Then I looked up and saw the fireworks!"

"All this chit-chat is really neat," Raphael butted in, with a quick glance sky-wards. "But if we don't get up there quick, this is going to turn into a mega disaster!"

"Raphael's right!" agreed Michaelangelo.

"Let's go, Turtles!" cried Leonardo, in command once more.

Inside, the whole building was like a frozen winter wonderland. The stairs were totally frozen over and icicles hung from the ceiling.

"We'll never get to the roof on that staircase!" declared Leonardo.

"Why walk," puffed Raphael, pulling hard at the doors to the lift, "when you can ride?"

"Forget it, dude!" advised Michaelangelo, peering down the lift shaft. "The elevator is frozen solid!"

"That's never stopped us Turtles before!" And like the true leader he was, Leonardo leapt at the lift cable and began climbing!

It took them only minutes to reach the souvenir shop at the top of the skyscraper. Shredder, Krang, Bebop and Rocksteady were gathered around their precious solar syphon.

"In a matter of minutes," Shredder was saying, "the solar batteries will be full and we shall be the absolute rulers of the Earth!"

"You want to double check that timetable?" challenged Raphael. The villains whirled round. Shredder gave a growl of fury.

"The Turtles! Get them!"

"Easier said than done!" taunted Raphael, as Bebop and Rocksteady came charging towards them. "Let's give them a few souvenirs!"

In seconds the Turtles had snatched up all the strings of beads and joke light bulbs on

display and flung them down, sending the
two morons skidding across the floor.

"Hey!" grunted Rocksteady. "Who turned
on the lights?"

"You wretched reptiles!" stormed Krang.
"I'll stop you!"

But Raphael was already at the far end of
the counter, tipping up the end of a long
shelf laden with statuettes, clocks and china
dolls. Krang all but disappeared under the
tacky heap.

"I'll fix you!" snarled Shredder, beside
himself with rage. Leonardo darted
forward, drawing his sword.

"Care to tangle with this Turtle?" he
demanded. Shredder dodged back behind a
huge steel post.

Leonardo lashed out, but hit the post instead, slicing it in half with his sword. Shredder just managed to leap away as it fell to the ground with a tremendous clang.

"Now, to turn the heat back on!" cried Donatello, working the controls of the solar syphon, while Leonardo, Raphael and Michaelangelo closed in on the villains.

"We're surrounded!" shouted Shredder, with a flair for stating the obvious. "Emergency escape!"

And before the Turtles could move, Shredder, Krang, Rocksteady and Bebop had crashed straight through the window!

"What the heck...?" gasped Raphael, taken completely off guard. He followed Leonardo to the window, just in time to see four parachutes billowing out below them.

"Have a nice day!" Shredder called to them.

"We've got to follow them!" yelled Michaelangelo.

"Only we'll take the stairs!" shouted Leonardo.

It certainly was an easier way down! The only thing missing was a toboggan for a three-man Teenage Mutant Hero Turtle team!

"Cow-a-bunga-a-a-!" yelled Michaelangelo.

Donatello worked away on the controls of the solar syphon. "There!" he beamed. "Now all that energy is flowing back into the sun!"

Sure enough, the sun was becoming brighter and brighter, bigger and bigger. Soon its rays began warming the frozen buildings, melting the icicles and thawing the ice into puddles.

Gradually, the humming and the crackling of Shredder's solar syphon stopped. Everything was back to normal.

"Now," he continued, "to shut this thing down for always!" He raised his staff... And while he was busy smashing the solar syphon to bits, Leonardo, Raphael and Michaelangelo were studying a huge, smoking hole in the street - the hole which they knew had been left by Krang's transport module.

Leonardo could guess what the other two were thinking. "Don't worry, fellas!" he comforted. "One of these days we'll catch Shredder!"

Back at the underground lair, Master Splinter was waiting for them. "I hope this has taught you all a valuable lesson!" he said.

"It certainly has, Master," said Leonardo. "I learned not to let doubts get in the way of my duty."

"I learned that I need to trust my instincts as much as my inventions!" said Donatello.

"And I learned that it's easier to make jokes than decisions!" added Raphael.

"Excellent, my students!" Clearly, Master Splinter was very pleased. "And what did you learn, Michaelangelo?"

"That you've got to stick to what you do best!" And he began tucking into his favourite meatball and peanut butter pizza!